For perplexed parents everywhere - C.C.

First published in 2000 by Macmillan Children's Books, London
First dual language publication 2002 by Mantra Lingua
All rights reserved

Mantra Lingua
5 Alexandra Grove, London N12 8NU
www.mantralingua.com

ما با این بچّهٔ نا آرامی که همه اش
"بوو هوو" می کند چه کنیم؟

What Shall We Do With The BOO HOO BABY?

by Cressida Cowell

Illustrated by Ingrid Godon

Farsi translation by Parisima Ahmadi-Ziabari

Mantra Lingua

بچه کوچلو گفت،

The baby said,

„بوو – هوو – هوو!‟

"Boo-hoo-hoo!"

اردک گفت:
"کواک؟"

"Quack?"
said the duck.

ما با این بچّهٔ نا آرامی که همه اش
"بوو هوو" می کند چه کنیم؟

What shall we do with
the boo-hoo baby?

سگ گفت: "به او غذا بدیم."

"Feed him," said the dog.

So they fed the baby.

بنا براین به او غذا دادند.

گربه گفت:
"میو!"

"Miaow!"
said the cat.

بچّه گفت:

”بوو – هوو– هوو !“

"Boo-hoo-hoo!"
said the baby.

بچّه گفت:
”بوو – هوو‐ هوو !“

"Boo-hoo-hoo!"
said the baby.

ما با این بچّهٔ نا آرامی که همه اش بوو - هوو می کند چه کنیم؟
گاو گفت:
"با او بازی کنیم."

What shall we do with
the boo-hoo baby?
"Play with him,"
said the cow.

بنا براین با او بازی کردند.

So they played with the baby.

اردک گفت:
" کواک!"

"Quack!"
said the duck.

سگ گفت:
" بوو – وو!"

"Bow-wow!"
said the dog.

گربه گفت:
" مییوُ!"

"Miaow!"
said the cat.

گاو گفت:
"مووو!"
"Moo!"
said the cow,

و ...

and...

بچّه گفت:
"بوو – هوو– هوو !"

"Boo-hoo-hoo!"
said the baby.

ما با این بچّهٔ نا آرامی
که همه اش بوو – هوو
می کند چه کنیم؟
اردک گفت:
"او را توی تختش بگذاریم."

What shall we do with
the boo-hoo baby?
"Put him to bed,"
said the duck.

So they put him to bed.

گربه گفت:

"مییو!"

"Miaow!"
said the cat.

بنا براین او را توی تختش گذاشتند.

گاو گفت: اردک گفت: سگ گفت:

"مووو!" "کواک!" "بوو - وو!"

"Moo!"
said the cow,

"Quack!"
said the duck.

"Bow-wow!"
said the dog.

و....

and...

زززز بچّه گفت. ززززززززز

ZZZZZZZZZ said the baby.

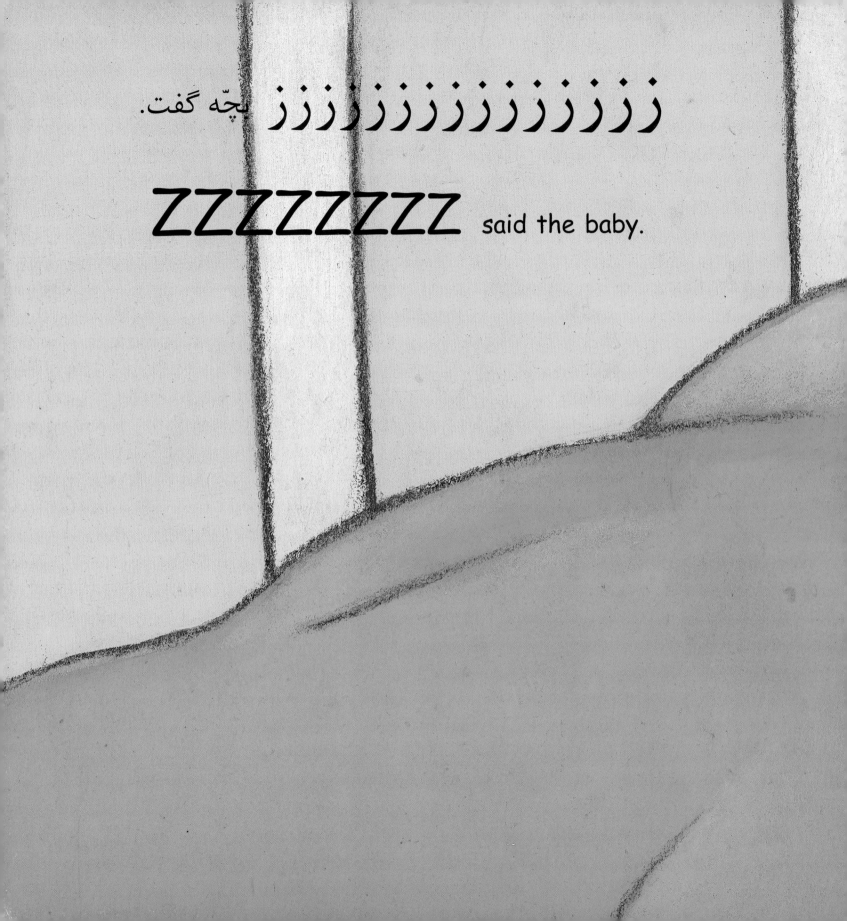

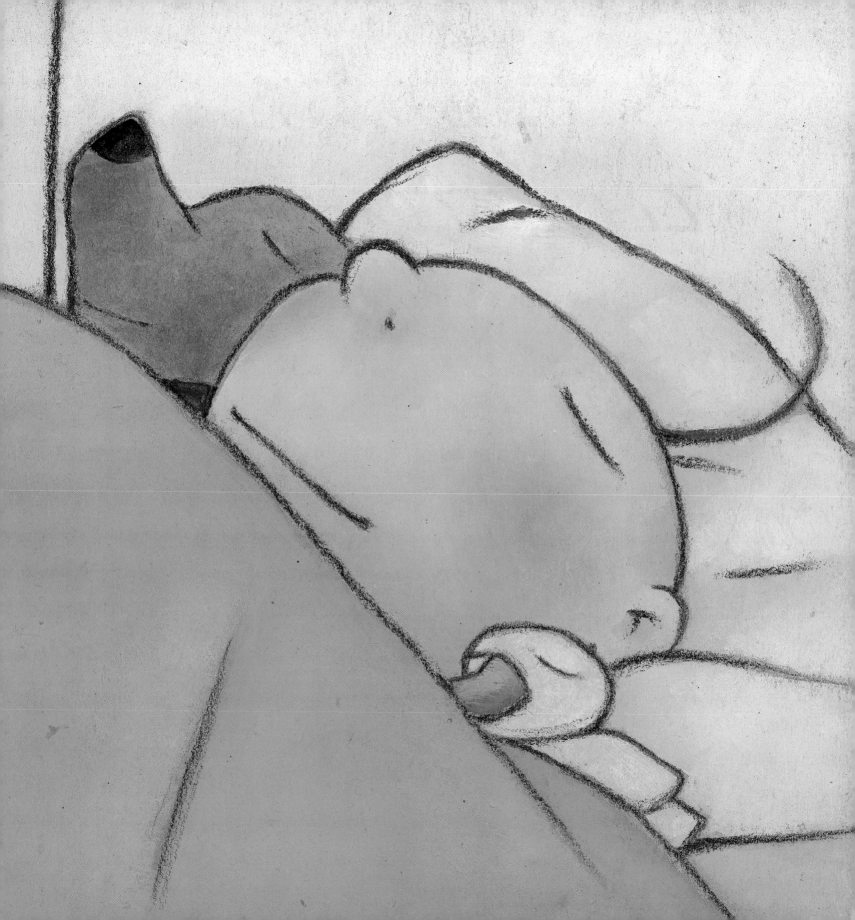